The Wishing Well Adventures

Book A: The Alamo

What's the Word, Thunderbird?

by Melissa Meadows
art by Melvyn Grant

Firelight Press

Library of Congress Cataloging-in-Publication Data
Meadows, Melissa.
What's the word, thunderbird? : A is for the Alamo / by
Melissa Meadows ; illustrations by Melvyn Grant. — 1st ed.
p. cm. — (The wishing well adventures ; bk. 1)
Summary: When nine-year-old Edgar and eight-year-old Brook
toss an enchanted penny into a hidden wishing well, they
unleash the spirit of American hero Davy Crockett, but also set
free a destructive ghost bird.

[1. Magic—Fiction. 2. Crockett, Davy, 1786-1836—Fiction.]
I. Grant, Melvyn, ill. II. Title.
III. Title: What is the word, thunderbird?
PZ7.M5075Wh 2007
[Fic]—dc22
2007019434

ISBN-13: 978-1-934517-00-0 (paperback)
ISBN-10: 1-934517-00-3 (paperback)

First Paperback Edition, Firelight Press

Published in the United States of America
Printed in Canada

Wishingwelladventures.com

Contents

What's the Word, Thunderbird?

Once Upon a Time

Davy Crockett stood on the wall of the Alamo fort. The air was cool on his face. It felt good. Later it might be icy again.

But it wasn't the ice that worried him. It was his dream.

A dream had woken him early, but now it was gone. He tried to remember it, but it blurred like the mist around him.

Davy looked at his pocket watch. It was five in the morning. He tried to see through the cool fog, but he could not.

Something in his dream made him look harder. The mists parted. Then he saw it.

A few pink sunrays lit the sky. Under them the horizon darkened as a huge army approached . . .

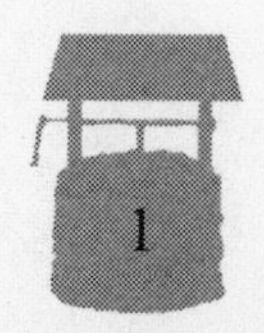

1

The Penny

Edgar watched the sunlight shine on the wet morning grass. It was the first day of summer. He knew this would be his best summer yet. There was only one problem. Edgar lived on a farm with no other kids nearby to play with.

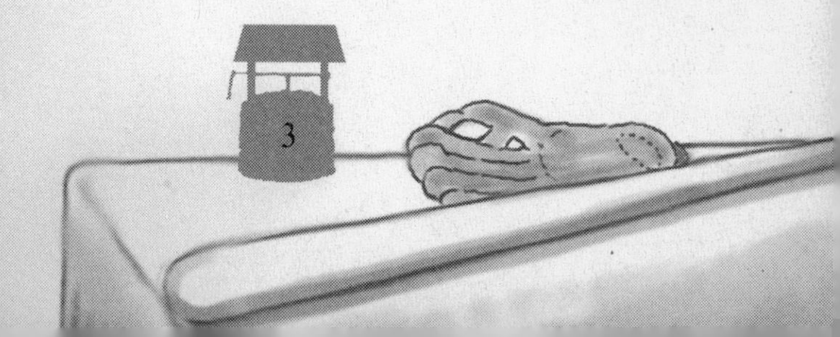

No other kids except one. And he did not want anything to do with Brook Thompson.

Brook was eight years old, and Edgar was nine. She was all right, Edgar thought, until she started talking about her uncle Sam.

Brook's stories about her uncle were crazy. Like how he visited a fairy country and became one inch tall. Come on.

No, Edgar was not in the mood for Brook and her stories. That's why he was not happy when his mother called him. "Edgar, come down. Brook is here to play."

Great. This was not how he wanted to start his best summer.

Brook looked happy to see him. "Guess what, Edgar? I got a letter from my uncle Sam!"

Edgar did not answer. He did not want to

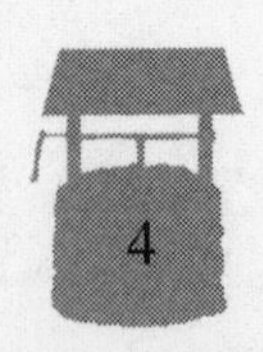

hear any more.

His mother frowned. “Edgar, aren’t you going to ask Brook about her letter?”

He made a face. “I don’t like letters.”

“Edgar!” His mother looked surprised. “That’s not polite.”

“All right,” Edgar said. It looked like he was stuck hearing another one of Brook’s stories. “What was the letter about?”

“My uncle visited the fairy kingdom again,” Brook said. “They made him really small. He lived under a mushroom in the grass there.”

Yeah, right, Edgar thought. And I’m the king of the lions.

“Guess what else?” Brook hopped on her toes, excited.

“What?”

“He sent me a special coin from the fairy

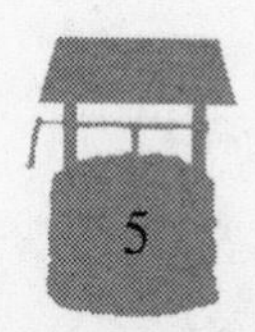

country. It's magic. You can hold it if you're really careful."

Her uncle sent a coin? Now Edgar was more interested. Could Brook really have fairy money? He held out his hand.

Brook handed a coin to Edgar. It was a shiny penny, the same as the ones in his piggy bank. This was not a fairy coin. Of course. Brook was making the whole thing up.

She looked at him, excited. "My uncle said it will take me on a magic adventure. I just have to find out what to do with it. Want to help me?"

Edgar's mother smiled at Brook's story. "Go ahead, Edgar," she said.

Edgar was stuck with Brook again. Slowly he followed her outside. She tossed the penny up in the air and caught it. "This thing will

give us the best summer ever," she said.

She threw it up again. This time the penny dropped onto the dirt. But instead of falling on its side, it rolled down the hill.

"How did it do that?" Edgar said. He and Brook chased the penny. It kept rolling all the way into the woods. It bounced over sticks. It skipped on rocks. Nothing stopped it.

Until the coin crashed into an old, stone well. That was odd. Edgar had never seen a well in these woods before.

2
The Well

Even though the stones of the well had crumbled, the rocks sparkled with pretty colors. A wooden roof let thin beams of sunlight through, making dancing patterns on the rim.

For a minute the well rippled in the light like a ghost. Then the sun went behind a cloud, and it was solid and normal again.

Brook was surprised. “I don’t remember

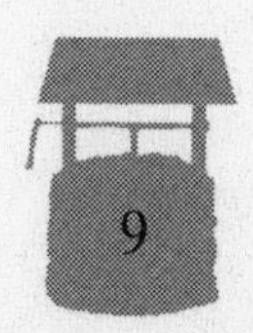

seeing this here before." She put the penny in her pocket.

They leaned over the stone wall of the well and looked down inside. They could see no water at the bottom, only darkness.

"Do you have a penny?" Brook asked. "Maybe if we threw it in the well, we could get a wish."

"You have a penny in your pocket, Brook. Remember?" Edgar said.

Brook frowned. "No way. I'm not losing my magic penny in this well."

"If it's really magic," Edgar said, "it might give you a wish."

Brook pulled the penny out of her pocket.

She looked back and forth between it and the well.

"I don't know," she said. "This is special. If I throw it in, I'll never get it back."

Edgar did not think the penny was special at all. Throwing it in the well was the best thing to do with it.

Then he had a good idea.

"Hey, look." He turned a handle on the well. The bucket went down. "You can put the penny in here. We'll drop it into the well, make a wish, and then pull it back out again."

Brook grinned. "Great idea!"

They put the penny in the bucket. Brook turned the handle until the rope hung all the way down into the well.

Edgar wondered what to wish for. He did

want a new bike. But Brook probably wanted something else. What would they both like?

Before they had a chance to talk about it, a strange cry came from the well.

"What was that?" Brook said. They looked inside.

A dark shadow moved deep inside the well. It squawked and shook. Then it banged against the walls.

Edgar did not know what it was. But it was big.

Then it rushed up, right at them.

"Watch out!" Edgar cried. He and Brook jumped back.

An enormous black bird flew out of the well. It shot straight up, filling the sky. Sparkling purple feathers lined its wings and chest. Its beak was gold.

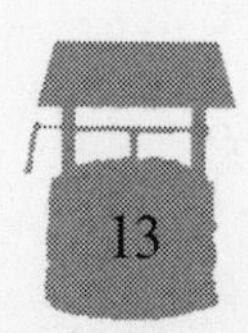

Everything grew dark. The bird hovered over them, so big it blocked the sun. The air got cold. Edgar shook all over. What was happening?

Brook pointed at the bird, shocked. Her lips moved but no words came out.

A white light shot out from behind the bird. It was bright, flashing, and it hit a tree with a loud crack.

Edgar turned to Brook, his mouth wide open. That bird had just made . . . lightning.

Emily N.

My favorite part was when the bird flew up out of the well and made lighting!

Andrew N

my favorite part was when Brooke was telling Edgar aboot her new coin!

3

In the Bucket

Edgar felt his heart pound like a drum. A second bolt of lightning struck the trees around them.

A branch caught on fire. It fell to the ground with a crash. Edgar and Brook stepped back in shock. Soon the dry leaves on the ground near them were burning.

The bird's wings fanned the fire, and the flames grew higher.

Just as they turned to run, rain began pouring from the sky. It put out the fire.

Edgar was confused. The sun had just been shining. The kids ran under a tree to keep dry.

The bird flew away, lightning shooting from its wings. All of a sudden the rain stopped.

"What was that?" Brook asked. "That bird made rain and lightning."

"It must have been magic," Edgar said. "But how? And why?"

Then he remembered the penny they had put in the bucket. Could it have turned into a bird? Could it really be magic?

Brook had the same thought. Both of them ran to the well and looked in.

Something was in the bucket, but it was not the penny. It looked furry.

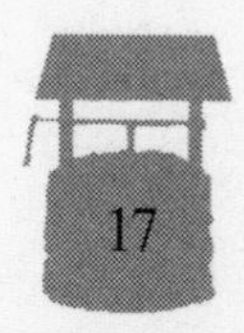

Edgar and Brook looked at each other. Should they pull it out of the well? What if it was something dangerous?

Brook bit her lip. “That penny was a gift from my uncle. I guess I can’t just leave it down there. Whatever it is now.”

She turned the handle on the well. Slowly, the bucket rose higher. When Brook got tired,

Edgar took a turn. He was afraid to see what they would pull up.

When the bucket got high enough, Brook grabbed it.

"Look." She reached in and pulled out an old wooden disc. It had a picture of a bird on one side and funny symbols carved into the other. A leather strap made it into a necklace.

"Cool!" Brook said. She put it around her neck.

Edgar looked into the bucket. On top of a pile of fur was a stone. It was carved into a triangle with a small handle.

"Look," he said. "It's an arrowhead."

Brook grabbed a piece of paper sticking out from the fur. "Maybe this will tell us what's going on." But it was only a recipe for apple pie.

"Huh?" Brook scratched her head. "Why is this in here?"

"I guess the penny is magic," Edgar said.

He could not believe that Brook was right. Her stories about her uncle Sam were so crazy. How could this be real?

Then he felt a chill. What if all those stories were true?

Brook yanked the fur out of the bucket.

"Look!" she said. "It's a coonskin cap!" She held it by its striped tail. Suddenly, the hat let out a shriek. Eyes popped open and claws sprung out. Brook dropped the furry thing, which now had turned into an angry raccoon.

"That was not necessary," it sniffed, nose in the air. "Did I grab you by your bottom?"

"Y . . . you talked!" Edgar said.

But before the raccoon could answer, it spun into the air, higher and higher, on a stream of mist.

"Watch out!" Edgar cried.

4

Davy Crockett

The raccoon blew above their heads, spinning around. A cloud of fog whirled with it.

When the fog disappeared away, a man stood near them. He held the raccoon in his hands. Both the man and the raccoon looked amazed.

"I can't believe it," the man said. "You saved me. Thank you."

"Who are you?" Brook asked.

"Don't you know?" the man said. "I'm Davy Crockett. Defender of the Alamo, famous frontiersman, and storyteller."

Edgar got it now. This was just a dream. He was not really here. There was no huge bird that made lightning. Davy Crockett was not standing in front of him.

Only he sure looked like he was.

Brook put her hands on her hips. "But Davy Crockett's not real."

"I'm very real, ma'am. Or at least I used to be. I was a hero of America's past, if I do say so myself." He dusted himself off. "Born in 1786 in Tennessee. I was in the Congress. That's the part of our government that makes laws."

Davy's voice grew quiet. "I tried to help

the squatters. They were the farmers out west who couldn't afford to buy land. And I gave my life at the Alamo so people could be free."

"What's the Alamo?" Edgar asked.

Davy said, "Back in 1836, the people of Texas wanted to be free from Mexico. So they fought for what they believed in a war called the Texas Revolution. The Alamo was an important battle."

Davy looked at the raccoon. "What happened to my hat? This used to be my coonskin cap. Look what that well did to it."

The raccoon put its hands on its hips. "Your hat? Ha! I'm the one who wears hats." It put on a small baseball cap and jumped out of Davy's hands.

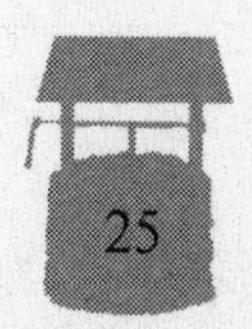

"But I need my hat back." Davy crossed his arms. He and the raccoon glared at each other.

The raccoon snorted. "Maybe I should wear a Davy skin hat," it said. It started to prance around, crossing its arms like Davy.

Davy said, "I know how to make you back into a cap."

The raccoon looked thoughtful. It rubbed its paws together. "All right. I'll sit on your head. But just for a while, and I'll wear my cap."

The raccoon jumped on top of Davy's head, and they both looked happy.

The kids stared in shock. "Why are you here?" Brook asked.

"I don't know," Davy Crockett said. "Feels

like I was stuck in that well forever. Not my body, you know. It was my spirit that was trapped. You should see all the people and things inside that well. From all over the country too."

Davy frowned. "I don't know who's behind this. Seems like someone has captured the entire heart of America in there."

This man seemed real to Edgar. Could he actually be Davy Crockett? "Why were you famous?" he asked.

Davy grinned and sat on a log. "Because I did it all. I was a sharpshooter, an explorer, a hunter. I wrote a book about myself. Killed a bear when I was only three. And I told the best stories both sides of the Mississippi."

Making up stories. That sounded just like Brook. Edgar gave him a hard look.

"Well, okay," Davy Crockett said. "Maybe I didn't kill the bear. But the rest is true."

The raccoon took off its cap, put on a sleeping bonnet, and curled up for a nap on Davy's head.

"But why are you here now?" Brook asked.

"I don't rightly know," Davy said. "You got me out of that well somehow. But something is still holding me here." He looked around. "How did you do it?"

"We put a magic penny in the well," Edgar said. "Then a huge bird flew out, with lightning coming from its wings."

Davy's face turned white. "No. Don't tell me that thing escaped too. That thunderbird has wild blood. It'll destroy everything here."

“Everything?” Edgar asked.

“You and you,” he said. “And me. Everything.”

5

The Secret Code

Davy Crockett tried to explain. "The thunder-bird isn't real now, any more than I am. It's a ghost bird, a part of America's past. It was fine in the well, where it was trapped. But you don't want it out here." Davy looked around with a frown.

"Why not?" Edgar asked. He had a bad feeling he knew why, though. That bird was scary.

Davy rested his chin on his fists. "It's the bird of storms, of fire in the night sky. It was the only legend that almost all of the American Indian tribes shared. They loved it, but they were afraid of it too."

"So, what can we do?" Edgar asked.

"We'll hunt it down and catch it, of course," Davy said. "What weapons do you have?"

Brook giggled. "None."

"I have a slingshot at home," Edgar said. "But it doesn't really work."

Davy couldn't believe it. "What kind of frontier kids are you, anyway?"

"Well," Edgar said, "this isn't the frontier anymore."

Davy looked around the woods. "So where is the frontier now?"

Brook said, "It's gone. There are cities

everywhere. All the way out to California."

Davy whistled. "There must be wagon trains all over the place."

Edgar laughed. "We ride in cars now. They take us places faster, without horses."

Davy grinned. "You like tall tales, too, don't ya? Anyway, we better catch this thunderbird before it causes real trouble. What do you all have on you?"

"Just what we got from the well," Brook said.

They held out the arrowhead, necklace, and apple pie recipe in their hands. They could not use any of these things.

Davy looked at the wooden necklace. He pointed at the picture of the bird. "That's the symbol for the thunderbird," he said. Then he turned it over and laughed. "Well, look at

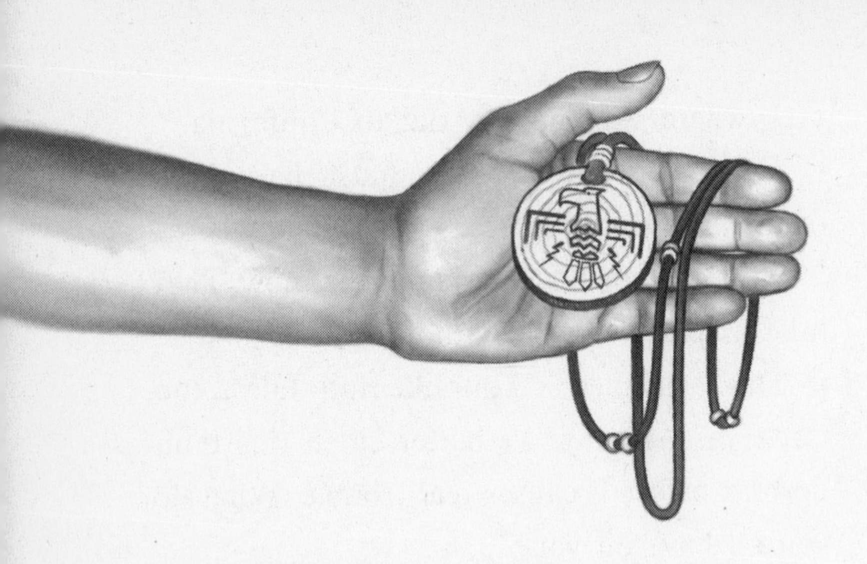

that. Symbols from the Cherokee tribe. This might be our answer right here."

The kids stared at the strange marks carved into the wood.

Davy said, "This means 'rain dance.' Maybe we can catch the thunderbird with a rain dance."

"The letters are beautiful," Brook said. "They're like a secret code."

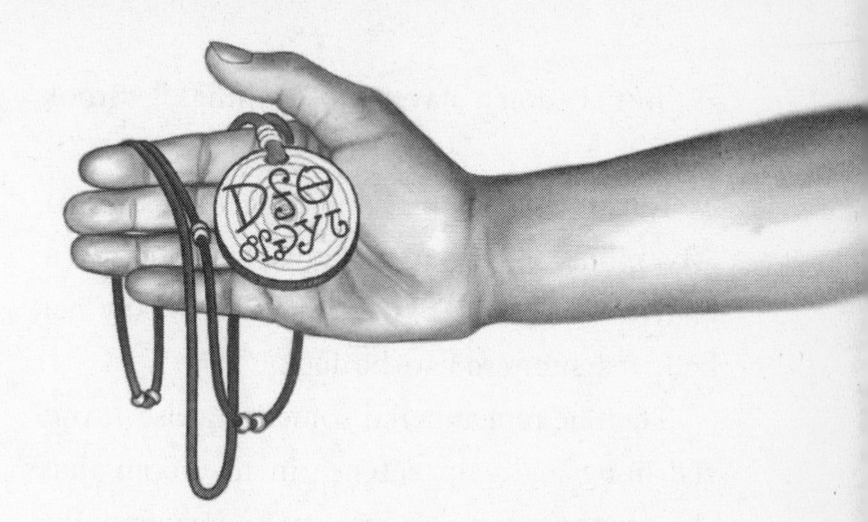

"Yup," Davy nodded. "A Cherokee man named Sequoya made their alphabet out of syllable sounds instead of letter sounds."

"How do we do a rain dance?" Brook asked.

"You asked the right person," Davy said. "An old Indian friend taught me. In order for it to work we need feathers for wind and turquoise for rain."

"But I don't have those things," Brook said.

Edgar rubbed his hands together, excited. "My mom bought a turquoise bracelet at a Native American festival. She keeps it by her bed. It's supposed to be lucky."

Then he remembered something else. "And she hung a dream catcher in my room that she got there too. It's supposed to catch nightmares, so I'll only have good dreams. That has feathers on it."

"Perfect." Davy smiled. "We'll bring down that bird with a rain dance. Then I'll figure out what to do with it. Run along and get your feathers and turquoise, kids. I'll wait here."

Edgar was smiling. Catching a thunderbird sounded like fun. As long as it wasn't too dangerous.

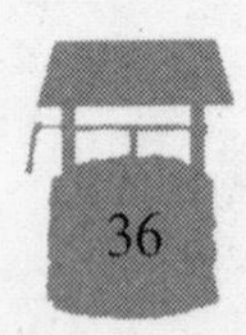

6

Thunderbird Damage

They ran up the hill to Edgar's house. What had started as a boring day was now the best ever. They had met Davy Crockett, seen a thunderbird, and were going to learn a real rain dance.

Suddenly, the sky darkened. The thunderbird flew over them. It blocked out the sun.

Lightning shot from its wings. Rain fell from its body.

The kids stopped. A bolt of lightning crackled into the ground nearby.

They screamed and ran into Edgar's house.

Edgar's mom smiled when she saw them. "I'm glad you two are having fun."

Edgar wondered if he should ask to borrow her bracelet. He only needed it for a few minutes. Then he would put it right back.

"What's this?" Edgar's mother took the paper out of his hand. He forgot he had been holding the apple pie recipe.

"Hmm. This looks good. Where did you get this?" she asked.

Edgar said, "I found it in a well."

His mother was not paying attention. She

began to look through the refrigerator for apples.

She said, "I've been wanting to make apple pie. You must have found one of my mother's old recipes. I wish I could find her other ones."

"We're going back out."

Edgar's mother turned around. "I don't think it's a good idea for you two to go outside again."

She said, "The weather has been strange this morning. I was worried about you two out there. Did you see what happened to the old silo?"

Edgar shook his head. The silo was the tall building where the farmers used to store their corn.

"I couldn't believe it," his mother said. "It

got dark, and lightning was flashing. I looked out and saw the old silo was on fire. The lightning must have hit it. Then rain started pouring down."

She looked worried. "The rain stopped the fire pretty fast. But half the silo had burned down. It's a good thing we don't use that one now."

Edgar's stomach sank. The silo burned down!

His mother put her head in her hand. "And then our car got dented from hail."

This was his fault. If he hadn't put that penny in the well, it would not have happened.

That was it. Edgar had to stop the thunderbird before it caused any more problems.

7

Feathers and Turquoise

"We'll be fine, Mom," Edgar said. "It's sunny now, see? We'll come in if it gets bad."

He ran upstairs and took his mother's turquoise bracelet and his dream catcher. Then he and Brook ran back to the woods.

Davy Crockett sat where they had left him, drawing in the dirt with a stick. "It feels

good to be out of that well," he said. "It was clammy in there."

The raccoon was making small piles of leaves and rolling in them.

"We need to catch this thunderbird," Edgar said. "It burned down the old silo on our farm."

Davy shook his head. "I learned some rain dances from my American Indian friends. We can try one and see if it works."

"Did you know a lot of Native Americans?" Brook asked.

"I got to know some on the frontier. Fought as hard as I could against what President Andrew Jackson did to them. Too bad I couldn't stop him. It led to the Trail of Tears."

Edgar asked, "What was the Trail of Tears?"

Davy Crockett patted his own head and the raccoon jumped up on top of it.

"No country is perfect," he said. "One of the things that makes ours great is we can look back and honestly talk about what we've done wrong. In a lot of countries, people can't do that.

"President Jackson made the Indians leave their homes and move west of the Mississippi River. A lot of them died."

Suddenly, the wind knocked Davy right off his log. Edgar grabbed the dream catcher, and the raccoon caught the bracelet before it blew away. The sky grew dark and the air got cold.

"It's back," Davy whispered.

Edgar looked up at the shadow of the thunderbird in the sky. Lightning shot from its wings.

"Now's our chance," Davy said. "Do you have the feathers and turquoise?"

The raccoon dusted itself off and proudly gave Brook the bracelet. He cleared his throat a few times until she thanked him. Edgar held the dream catcher. Davy took the arrowhead. It sparkled in his hand.

"This is going to work," Davy said. "I can tell. We just need to get it right."

Davy put the arrowhead in his pocket and said, “Now march with your left foot, then your right foot, along with me. Move forward only a little bit each time.

“Lift your right foot higher than your left. And lean forward with the rhythm.”

Edgar, Brook, and the raccoon lined up behind him. Davy chanted words and slapped his leg to make a beat.

Rain water, rain water
Rain water, rain water
Creek rain, thunder thunder
Mud rain, thunder thunder
Fog mist, muddy water

Every other word was loud and the next was quiet. Then he repeated the chant in Cherokee. “A-ga-na ama, a-ga-na ama . . .”

Edgar felt like a real Native American. He almost laughed watching the raccoon, who was now wearing a tiny feather headdress, patting its knees, and bouncing to the beat.

The rain dance was working. The sky grew darker. Rain began to fall, soaking them.

The thunderbird drew close. It stared down at them with sharp eyes.

Then a huge bolt of lightning shot right in front of them. The light was blinding and the ground shook.

Brook screamed and ran into the woods.

8
The Alamo

Edgar and Davy ran after her. The thunderbird flew away and the rain stopped. They were soaked.

"Are you okay?" Edgar asked Brook.

She nodded, shivering. "That was scary."

The raccoon jumped into her arms, trembling. "It's okay, Brookie," it said. "I'll protect you." It blinked at her from under a broad hat decorated with flowers.

Brook hugged the raccoon. “What is your name?” she said.

The little animal held itself up proudly. “I’m Winston Thurston Preston Dustin Bugle the fourth.” It shot Brook a grin. “But you can call me Winston Bugle.”

“Aww,” she said, patting its head. “I’ll call you Winnie.”

“You will not,” Winston Bugle straightened his back and dusted off his fur. “It’s Winston Bugle or nothing, missy.”

“I’m sorry,” Davy said to Brook. “I should have warned you. That thunderbird is going to play rough.”

He took Winston Bugle from Brook. “But the rain dance was working,” he said. “We better try it again. And quick, before the thunderbird does more harm.”

Davy looked worried. "I think something is holding it here, just like it's holding me. If it feels trapped it could really cause problems."

"I can't do it," Brook said. "I don't like that thing. Get him without me."

Davy frowned. "You two set it free. You both need to help for this to work."

"No." Brook shook her head.

Davy said, "I know. Being brave is not always easy." He held Winston Bugle out in his hands. "Let me show you a little about bravery," he said. "Come with me back to the Alamo. Just touch ole' Winston's hat."

"What?" Winston Bugle said. "Get off my hat!"

Winston Bugle tried covering it with his little hands, but Davy, Brook, and Edgar squashed his straw hat down onto his head.

As soon as they did, bubbles surrounded them, in every color. The bubbles looked like big jellybeans. Then, just as fast, they were gone.

The kids and Davy were standing in a dusty fort with high walls. The people in the fort looked sad. Nobody seemed to see them.

A young man was sitting on a barrel. He put his head in his hands. "We'll never make it," he said.

Another man agreed. "There are thousands of Mexican soldiers and less than two hundred of us."

A woman wiped a tear from her eye. "But we can't let them win. Texas has to be free."

A dark-haired man came up to them. "It won't be easy."

"That's Colonel William Travis," Davy whispered.

Colonel Travis said, "Our country is great because of our spirit and determination. I'll do what it takes. But each of us must choose."

He drew a line in the dirt with his sword. "Those prepared to give their lives in freedom's cause, come over to me."

The people looked scared. Each had to decide what to do. Slowly, they began to

cross the line. The young man who was sitting on the barrel bit his fingernails. He looked frightened.

But then the young man stood up. He lifted his chin proudly and crossed the line. Soon everyone had crossed.

Colored bubbles again surrounded Edgar and Brook. Suddenly they were back in the woods.

The kids thought about what they saw at the Alamo. They couldn't let the thunderbird stay here.

"I'll try the rain dance again," Brook said. "I can be brave like the people at the Alamo." She felt in her pocket. "Oh, no! I lost the bracelet."

Edgar could not believe it. Now he was really in trouble. He hadn't even asked his

mom if he could borrow it.

Davy shook his head. “I don’t know if the rain dance will work without the turquoise. All we can do is try.”

Davy frowned. “When that bird gets near us, you two stop dancing and clear off. I’ll finish the rain dance by myself until I can trap it.”

Edgar wondered how Davy would trap such a dangerous creature.

9

The Arrowhead

They walked back to the well. Davy said, "This time I want it to get really close. I'll chant louder. You two say 'ama, ama' along with my words. That means 'water, water.'"

They did the rain dance again. Their feet stepped high, low, high, low. Their voices went loud, quiet, loud, quiet.

Winston Bugle threw himself into the rhythm and chanted "ama, ama" with Edgar

and Brook.

Davy sung the rain dance words louder and drummed on his legs. They leaned back and forth to the beat.

Soon the thunderbird was above them. It looked angry. Rain began to fall.

"Keep going, kids," Davy said. "Just a little longer."

Lightning hit a tree. Burning branches fell in front of them. Hailstones as big as oranges dropped around their feet.

Then a huge lightning bolt shot right at Davy Crockett.

"Back away now, kids," Davy shouted. "It can't hurt me."

Edgar, Brook, and Winston Bugle ran under the trees. Davy chanted loud. He pounded his legs. "Rain water, rain water."

The thunderbird dove at him, sparks flying from its eyes. Davy pulled out the arrowhead. He reached back with it, squinting, like he might throw it.

The thunderbird shot another lightning bolt at Davy. It zapped through him.

"Did you see that?" Edgar whispered.

"I guess Davy's okay because he's not alive anymore," Brook said. Winston Bugle covered his face with his paws.

The thunderbird dipped down toward the well. Its eyes glowed. When it got very close to the well, a blue fog glowed around it. The fog seemed connected to both the bird and the well.

Davy walked to the well. When he got close enough the strange blue fog covered him too, attaching him to the well.

Davy whooped and jumped in the air. "Look! I can see it now. This is what's holding us here!"

He sliced the arrowhead into the blue haze between the bird and the well. The arrowhead cut through the fog like magic. Blue steam shot from under the blade. Davy sawed through the mist. Soon, the bird was cut free from the magic that held it there. It burst high into the air.

The thunderbird swirled in the sky. It dropped something small in front of Edgar's feet and—poof!—it vanished.

10

Freedom

Edgar looked on the ground. The thunderbird had dropped a small packet of white, glittery stars. He picked it up.

"Whoopee!" Davy shouted. "It's free! I can cut myself loose too." He stepped close to the well and the fog around him came back. "This is what is keeping me here. Now I can set my spirit free."

He sat on the log. "There is only one problem."

"What's that?" Edgar asked. He couldn't think of any problems. The thunderbird was gone. The sun was shining. Everything was back to normal. If only he had his mother's bracelet.

Davy said, "Other spirits are trapped in that well. I hate to leave them in there."

He scratched his head and then smiled at the kids. "But you got me out, and the thunderbird. If I go free, will you try to help the others down there?"

"Yes!" Brook said.

Edgar nodded his head. He wanted to help.

"You'll need this then." Davy gave the arrowhead to Edgar. "Keep those stars that the thunderbird dropped. Maybe they're a clue."

Davy patted Winston Bugle's back. "It was nice knowing you kids. Thanks for

saving me."

Brook smiled. "Can you tell us what happened at the Alamo?"

"We held out for thirteen days," Davy said, "until they broke down the walls of our fort. Then in a half hour it was all over."

Edgar got the chills thinking about it. But Davy Crockett laughed, kicked his feet up, and fell backward off the log. "Remember the Alamo!" he shouted.

"Why should we remember it?" Brook asked.

Davy winked at her. "It's just another example of people willing to give everything for what they believe in. Freedom, ma'am."

They were quiet for a while, thinking about this idea. Davy climbed back onto the log. "And freedom is what this country is all about."

11
Apple Pie

Winston Bugle pranced back and forth by the well. "Look," he said. "No blue mist. I'm not held here by anything. I can go wherever I want."

The magic fog surrounded Davy when he stepped close to the well. Edgar sliced through it with the arrowhead. Davy waved goodbye, and then he was gone.

They heard a scratching sound in the

$1/2

trees nearby. Edgar saw a shadow go into the woods, but he couldn't tell what it was.

"I think we better head back home," he said.

On the way back, Winston Bugle jumped up on Edgar's shoulder.

"Missing something?" Winston Bugle asked. He held up the turquoise bracelet that belonged to Edgar's mother.

"You found it! Thanks, Bugle!"

"Winston Bugle, that is." The raccoon crossed his arms. "Anyway, small eyes are the sharpest." He sniffed. "Yum. And my small nose is telling me something too."

The scent of apple pie came through the kitchen window. "I'll toss you out a piece," Edgar told him.

When Edgar and Brook came in, Edgar's

mother clapped her hand over her heart. "There you are. When the weather got bad again I went to call you in, but I couldn't find you."

She sat down. "You better play inside the rest of the day."

Edgar laughed. "It's okay now, Mom. You see, we let a thunderbird out of the well. It made the rain and lightning. But Davy Crockett set it free with an arrowhead. So we're all safe now."

His mother smiled at him like he was a very little child. "That sounds like a nice game. But I want you to stay inside now. Have some pie."

Edgar and Brook looked at each other. Did he really think his mother would believe that crazy story? He wasn't sure he even believed it.

He tossed a piece of pie out the window. Winston Bugle gobbled it up, waved, and then ran back into the woods.

Edgar put his hand in his pocket. He felt the arrowhead and the bag of stars. There were spirits in the well, and he would have to get them out.

Who had put them there?

He and Brook would have to find out.

In the meantime, the apple pie was delicious.

Glossary

The Alamo A church that later became a fort in the **Texas Revolution**. On March 6, 1836, the Mexican army broke into the Alamo fort. Fewer than two hundred brave Texans fought and died for freedom here against two thousand Mexican soldiers.

Andrew Jackson The seventh president of the United States, born in 1767. He was a military hero from the War of 1812 and was considered a spokesman for the common man. He made the office of president more powerful, like it is today.

Apple Pie Yum . . . so traditional and so good. This dish was popular in America since the time

of the settlers. Many think Americans perfected it. Do you like yours with cheddar cheese or ice cream?

Arrowheads Stones, metal, or bone chipped into a point or triangle and used for hunting. In this country they were usually Native American artifacts.

Congress The branch of government that makes the laws we all live by. It is made up of the House of Representatives and the Senate.

Davy Crockett Born in 1786, David Crockett led a life of adventure. He left home as a teenager and traveled through Tennessee, where he learned to be a great hunter, sharpshooter, and trapper. He spent time in the military and then served in the Congress for six years, fighting for squatters' rights and against the Indian Removal Act. Davy gave his life in the Battle of the Alamo.

Dream Catcher A willow hoop with a net in the center, often decorated with feathers and beads. Dream catchers are a symbol of unity between different Indian tribes and are said to catch nightmares, while letting good dreams pass through.

Frontier The wilderness beyond cities and towns. America was settled first in the east. The frontier moved further west as more people settled there.

Indian Removal Act Signed into law by President Jackson on May 28, 1830. It let the president exchange land that the Native Americans owned for unsettled land west of the Mississippi River. These exchanges were supposed to have been agreed upon by the Native American tribes, but these agreements were often questionable.

Sequoya A Cherokee man born in 1767. He spent twelve years inventing a Cherokee alphabet. It was called a syllabary because there was a separate character for each syllable sound—all eighty-six! For instance, Θ symbolizes the sound "na."

Squatters In the early 1820s, western land cost more than most people could afford. People weren't allowed to buy less than 320 acres from the government. Many people, called squatters, settled

the West, setting up homesteads and farming land they didn't own. The Homestead Act of 1862 gave squatters 160 acres of land for free.

The Texas Revolution In the 1830s, Texas was part of Mexico. The Mexican government worried that the people there might want to become a part of the United States. The Mexican government sent soldiers to keep out more American settlers and collect new taxes that the Texans did not want to pay. In the end, the Texans decided to fight for their freedom from Mexico. Later, Texas became part of the United States.

Thunderbird The only Native American icon that is common to almost all tribes. Makers of storms, thunderbirds were both worshipped and feared.

Trail of Tears On May 26, 1838, soldiers commanded by President Jackson made the Cherokee Tribe leave their homes and move far away, west of the Mississippi River. About four thousand Cherokees died. Other tribes were also forced to move west.

A is for Apples

By Kelsey J., 8 years old, Cincinnati, Ohio

Once there was a young man. His name was Johnny Appleseed. He went around America and planted apple seeds.

Now I'm going to tell a little story about Johnny. When Johnny was five he would only eat apples. He ate at least four hundred a day. When he was six he decided to travel around America. When he was seven he decided he wanted to plant apple seeds.

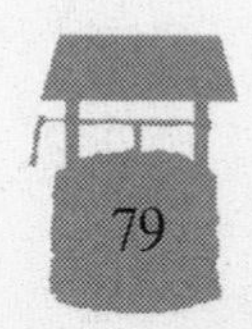

When he was twenty he went to Texas. That's where I was on vacation. I was down by the river drinking water when I saw Johnny Appleseed. Back then I thought he was a strange man with a pan on his head.

He saw me and walked up to me and said, "Would you like to go and . . ."

I interrupted. "I ain't goin' nowhere. I have to get to the wagon before the sun sets. Because I got to move."

Johnny planted an apple seed. The seed, in the heat and next to the river, grew very quickly into a tree. Johnny and I climbed up in the tree and ate some apples while we continued our conversation.

He asked, "Where you movin'?"

I answered, "To a farm in Idaho."

"Hey, that's where I'm goin' next!" he said.

I fell out of the tree and hung onto a branch. Johnny was too far away to catch me. He thought if he climbed out further to catch me the branch would break. So he broke off a branch and held it out to me. I grabbed onto it and I was safe.

I asked, “Where is your wagon?”

He answered, “I don’t have one. I travel on foot. Anyway, we’re talking about ourselves but don’t even know our names. I’m Johnny, but people call me Johnny Appleseed.”

“I’m Kelsey. Oh, no. It’s almost sunset. I have to go. See ya!”

The end.

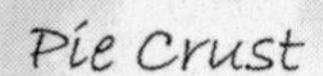

Pie Crust

3 cups all-purpose flour

1½ cups butter (3 sticks)

1 tablespoon sugar

1 pinch salt

3 tablespoons ice water

This is easiest in a food processor. Put in the cold butter, chopped into chunks, flour, sugar, and salt. Chop on high until it looks like small peas. Slowly add the water—two tablespoons at first, and a third if needed—while the food processor is going, until it turns into a ball of dough. This can also be done in an electric mixer or by hand.

A is for Apple Pie

¼ cup sugar
¼ cup brown sugar
¼ teaspoon allspice
¾ teaspoon cinnamon
3 tablespoons flour
1 teaspoon vanilla
3 pounds apples, chopped and peeled
1 pie crust, made or bought

-Mix ingredients and put in crust. Cover with top crust and cut slits in it. Pinch the edges together or press with a fork. Brush with sugar water and bake at 425 degrees for fifty minutes. Enjoy!

Your story could appear in a Wishing Well Adventures book!

Go to WishingWellAdventures.com and upload a story you have written that has to do with America. The title should begin with an upcoming letter of the alphabet. ("A Is for Apple Pie" or "B Is for Betsy Ross.") Your story will appear on our Web site, and it may be selected to be printed in the back of an upcoming Wishing Well book!